THE TROUBLE WITH GIRLS

Will Jacobs & Gerard Jones • Writers

Tim Hamilton • Penciller

Dave Garcia • Inker

Diane Valentino • Letterer

Tim Hamilton • Cover Illustration

Bruce Timm • Cover Coloring

Jim Chadwick • Logo Design

Dave Olbrich • Publisher

Chris Ulm • Editor-In-Chief

Tom Mason • Creative Director

Material in this collection was previously published
in comic book form by Malibu Graphics, Inc.
The Trouble With Girls #1 (August 1987)
The Trouble With Girls #2 (September 1987)
The Trouble With Girls #3 (October 1987)

ETERNITY PUBLISHING
Newbury Park, CA

Other books by Will Jacobs & Gerard Jones
The Beaver Papers
The Comic Book Heroes

Other books by Dave Garcia (with Monica Sharp)
Panda Khan

THE TROUBLE WITH GIRLS
Graphic Novel
Volume One
Published by
Eternity Comics
a division of Malibu Graphics, Inc.
1355 Lawrence Drive #212
Newbury Park, CA 91320
805/499-3015

$7.95/$9.95 in Canada
ISBN #0-944735-08-8

Scott Rosenberg/President
Chris Ulm/Vice-President
Tom Mason/Secretary
Dave Olbrich/Treasurer

INTRODUCTION
Paul Chadwick

I remember reading, once, a character description of Goofy that the Disney people worked up. Along with similar descriptions of other characters, it was intended as a guide to the animators as they drew Goofy going about his business. With it they could gauge every movement, reaction and body attitude so that Goofy would be consistently "in character." It's the same process an actor goes through to "build" his character, but in this case it was important to set it in print, so that any number of animators could stay faithful to the true Goofy.

What struck me was that the description covered not only Goofy's habits and traits, but also the behavior of the environment around him. It described how objects he touched would change to thwart him: solid ladders would turn to rubber, a car would only grudgingly, fitfully respond to his turning the wheel and stomping on the gas. It was as if he radiated an energy which gave life—and a subversive attitude—to the inanimate objects around him.

Will Jacobs and Gerard Jones have invoked a similar principle with their character Lester Girls. But Girls' aura draws from the environment not slapstick frustration, but danger, sex and wealth.

Men either throw sweepstakes prizes or bombs at him, and women throw themselves. Fortunately for Lester, a cool competence allows him to cope with all this without so much as skinning his knuckles. The result is that he lives a life that James Bond would find impossibly glamorous.

This could make for a fine satire in itself, but Jacobs and Jones have something else up their sleeves. Lester doesn't *want* any of this. He abhors glamour and excitement. He yearns for a secure, unsurprising nine-to-five and a mousey little wife to watch TV with. It's the Walter Mitty pancake flipped over and stuck to the ceiling. What's more, it makes for a character at war with his nature, and from that can be wrought the sort of humor that I like best—the kind that springs from a character's pain.

Not that there isn't a great deal of other humor to be found here. Jacobs and Jones specialize in throwaway gags, from the nicely understated (Girls casually tossing an assassin's corpse out the window prior to cocktails) to the occasionally groan-inducing (as when Maxi asks to speak to the "chief"). Tim Hamilton sneaks in a lick here and there, too, as when Girls is shot from a circus cannon and assumes the classic Wayne Boring flying Superman pose. Credit must also be given to Hamilton for Girls' cow-catcher jaw-line. A more communicative character design hasn't been seen.

So, prepare yourself for a romp, one with elements of parody, but with enough internal consistency to create a world of its own. This is a series pleasingly apart from the comics mainstream (although it is easily accessible), with its own distinct voice. It is thoughtfully silly, at turns droll and nasty and mockingly dramatic. I can't think of anything quite like *The Trouble With Girls*. You might say it takes a unique angle of attack.

Paul Chadwick
June, 1988

(Paul Chadwick is the creator/writer/artist of Concrete, *published bi-monthly by Dark Horse Comics.)*

I WAS ON THE EDGE OF MY SEAT.

BILLY BUCK WAS JUST ABOUT TO SHOW JODY HOW TO TRAIN THE PONY ON A LONG HALTER. BOY, THAT STEINBECK SURE KNEW HOW TO BUILD SUSPENSE.

I FLIPPED THE PAGE WITH TREMBLING FINGERS. AND *THAT'S* WHEN I HEARD THE TRUCK.

MEETING GIRLS

②

I RECOGNIZED THE DEAD ARAB KID ON MY LIVING ROOM RUG. HE SHOULD'VE LISTENED TO HIS KINDLY PARENTS.

OUTSIDE, THE RAIN WAS A TORRENT. IT SEEMED NATURAL, THOUGH. I DIDN'T THINK THE RUSSIANS WERE BEHIND IT THIS TIME.

GEARY AND LOMBARD!

TAXI

AS FAR AS I COULD MAKE OUT, ONLY FOUR CARS WERE FOLLOWING US.

I GOT OUT, ZIGZAGGED THROUGH UNION SQUARE...

RAN THROUGH THE HYATT, CAME OUT ON THE CHINATOWN SIDE, AND FLAGGED ANOTHER CAB.

SCREEEEECH

SHE SHRUGGED.

HOW ABOUT A *WALLBANGER*, LES?

NOT NOW. I WANT TO READ.

YOU WANT TO *WHAT*, HONEY?

I DIDN'T WANT AN ARGUMENT, SO I WENT INTO THE BEDROOM. I'D LOST MY BOOK, BUT I ALWAYS KEPT A COPY OF WHATEVER I'M READING IN ALL MY HOUSES, JUST IN CASE. TROUBLE WAS, IT TOOK ME 10 MINUTES TO FIND MY PLACE.

DAMNED ARABS.

THANKFULLY, THE BEAUTIFUL BIG-BREASTED REDHEAD LEFT ME ALONE FOR A WHILE. SHE TURNED THE RADIO ON AND BLARED DAVID LEE ROTH AT ME, BUT AT LEAST SHE DIDN'T BARGE INTO THE ROOM IN THE BUFF.

I FOUND THE PART ABOUT JODY AND THE LONG HALTER, BUT THE TRUCK-BOMB HAD ANNOYED ME SO MUCH I COULDN'T CONCENTRATE. AFTER READING THE SAME LINE 3 TIMES I GAVE UP.

THERE WERE SIX CARS STAKED OUT DOWN THERE NOW. HOW DID I KNOW THEY DIDN'T JUST BELONG TO MY NEIGHBORS, YOU ASK? DON'T. IT'S TOO HARD TO EXPLAIN.

MEANWHILE, IN CHINA...

THE BUNGALOW!

OH, MAGNIFICENT ONE! PLEASE! PLEASE TARRY FOR ONE MORE BOUT OF ECSTASY! THIS ONE'S ON THE HOUSE!

YES! IN GRATITUDE FOR ALL YOU HAVE TAUGHT US.

GOTTA GET TO THE BUNGALOW.

PLEASE, OH GLORIOUS ONE. BE NOT A FOOL.! THE ENTIRE RED ARMY AWAITS IN AMBUSH FOR YOU!

BUNGALOW!

'TIS PASSING STRANGE!

THE REDHEAD WAS DANCING BY HERSELF IN THE MIDDLE OF MY NAVAJO RUG.

DID YOU CHANGE YOUR MIND ABOUT THAT DRINK, HONEY?

I'VE BEEN A PUPPET, A PAUPER, A PIRATE, A POET...

WHY THE HELL NOT?

I'LL BET A BIG GUY LIKE YOU LIKES HIS DRINKS STRONG.

JUST MAKE IT SNAPPY, SISTER.

SHE KICKED OFF HER SHOES, BUT EVEN THEN SHE ALMOST CAME UP TO MY CHIN. SHE WAS A BIG GIRL.

BIG, AREN'T I?

I WAS JUST THINKING THAT.

BOTTOMS UP.

TASTE IT.

WHAT?

YOU HEARD ME.

LAST TIME ONE OF THESE GIRLS GAVE ME A WALLBANGER, APACHE DICK HAD TO PUMP MY STOMACH FOR A DAY AND A HALF.

AND THEN THE LIGHTS WENT OUT.

WHAT DO YOU WANT, ANYWAY? HOW BIG DOES IT HAVE TO BE? DO YOU WANT HITLER TO TURN UP AS THEIR BUTLER?

I WANT *GIRLS*, OSCAR. *GIRLS.*

NEW YORK, PLEASE.

WHAT IS IT WITH YOU AND GIRLS? WHAT'S SO SPECIAL *ABOUT* GIRLS? THIS OBSESSION OF YOURS IS DOWNRIGHT UNNATURAL.

IT'S UNNATURAL FOR A HIGH-POWERED REPORTER TO BE OBSESSED BY THE BIGGEST STORY IN THE WORLD TODAY? MARTIN BORMANN IS NOSTALGIA, OSCAR. HE'S BIG BAND ERA, HE'S PADDED SHOULDERS. GIRLS IS *NOW!*

HOW CAN YOU *SAY* THAT? WHO KNOWS EVEN THE FIRST THING ABOUT GIRLS? AS FAR AS I'M CONCERNED, GIRLS IS JUST A RUMOR.

GIRLS IS AS REAL AS I AM, OSCAR. I'VE HEARD TOO MANY *REPORTS* OF HIS EXPLOITS, TOO MANY LEGENDS OF HIS *CONQUESTS* TO DISMISS HIM AS A MASS HALLUCINATION.

WELL, MAYBE NOT A HALLUCINATION. BUT HOW ABOUT A HOAX OR A RUSE?

HOW COULD *ONE* MAN OVERTHROW A LATIN DICTATOR ONE DAY, THEN CONTAIN A NUCLEAR MELTDOWN THE NEXT, AND STILL HAVE TIME TO DISCOVER PROOF THAT SHAKESPEARE WROTE ALL OF BACON'S ESSAYS?

NEW YORK? DAILY GAZETTE-CHRONICLE-PLANET-BEE, PLEASE.

THINK ABOUT IT, MAXI. IF A MAN LIKE THAT *DOES* EXIST, WHY DOESN'T HE STEP INTO THE SPOTLIGHT? HE COULD BE THE BIGGEST HERO IN THE WORLD. WHY DOESN'T HE COME FORWARD?

YOU JUST HIT THE NAIL ON THE HEAD, OSCAR. *THAT'S* THE STORY. WHY *DOESN'T* HE?

HE TURNED DOWN MULTI-MILLION DOLLAR CONTRACTS TO STAR IN A BLOCKBUSTER FILM STORY OF HIS LIFE. HE'S REFUSED TO TAKE THE REINS OF THE CIA AND THE FBI AGAIN AND AGAIN.

AND THERE'S YOUR STORY, OSCAR. IS THERE SOMETHING *WRONG* WITH HIM? IS HE HIDING SOMETHING? IS HE UP TO SOMETHING HE SHOULDN'T BE? WHO *IS* LESTER GIRLS?

HELLO? MAXI SCOOPS HERE. GIMME THE CHIEF.

HE EVEN REFUSED TO LET LEROY NIEMAN PAINT HIS PORTRAIT FOR THE COVER OF TIME. EVEN THAT.

BUT MAXI! WHAT ABOUT MARTIN BOR...

NO, NOT YOU, RUNNING BULL. I WANT THE *EDITOR.*

CHIEF HERE.

IN

OUT

DINGLE HERE.

LISTEN, BARRY. I FOUND BORMANN AND EARHART.

YOU WANT TO KNOW WHERE THEY ARE? GIVE ME THE LESTER GIRLS STORY AND THEY'RE YOURS. YES OR NO?

23

I THREW US BOTH TO THE FLOOR.

KEEP QUIET.

THEN MY EYES ADJUSTED TO THE DARK. I COULD SEE THEIR SILHOUETTES, CREEPING ALONG THE LEDGE, THEY MOVED AS SILENTLY AS CATS, THEIR KNIVES LIKE RAISED TAILS.

THE LLAMA COMMANCHE II .38 SPECIAL WITH THE HIGH-POLISH DEEP BLUE FINISH WAS WHERE I'D LEFT IT.

WHO... WHO ARE THEY, LES?

EVER HEAR OF THE SASHIMI BLADE?

THE WHAT?

SKIP IT.

THEY HAD DISAPPEARED. FOR NOW.

WHAT ARE YOU DOING?

COCKING MY REVOLVER.

LIE STILL. THEY MIGHT COME FROM ANYWHERE.

BLAM!
BLAM!

DUMBWAITER!

BLAM!

DON'T STOP.

I DIDN'T. THE SECOND ONE SWUNG THROUGH THE WINDOW.

BLAM!
BLAM!

I ONLY SPENT *TWO* SLUGS ON HIM BECAUSE THE RED-HEAD WASN'T GOING TO GIVE ME A CHANCE TO RELOAD.

AIEEEEEE

IT WAS ENOUGH.

DON'T STOP.

NO, LES. *NOT* FOUR NINJAS.

OH.

BY THE WAY, THEY'RE NOT NINJAS. THEY'RE *CHEFS*.

CHEFS?

YES. THE *SASHIMI BLADE*. AN ANCIENT ARCANE ORDER OF SUSHI CHEFS, WHO HAVE GUARDED THEIR SECRETS OF CULINARY MASTERY SINCE THE DAWN OF JAPAN'S HEIAN PERIOD.

BUT WHY ARE THEY AFTER YOU?

EVERYBODY'S AFTER ME, BUT MORE TO THE POINT, IT APPEARS THAT MY BLOOD-BROTHER, APACHE DICK, STOLE THEIR MOST REVERED SECRET: THE ART OF WRAPPING ALL THOSE LITTLE SALMON EGGS IN SEAWEED WITHOUT POPPING THEM.

THE DREAMY LOOK IN THOSE EYES FROZE ME.

I WORSHIP YOU, LESTER. YOU'VE TAUGHT ME WHAT IT MEANS TO LOVE. SUDDENLY I KNOW WHY THERE ARE SO MANY LOVE SONGS.

FORGET IT, BABE. I'M NOT THE GUY YOU THINK I AM. YOU WANT A GUY WHO CAN MAKE EXPERT LOVE TO YOU WHILE GUNNING DOWN NINJAS. THAT'S NOT ME.

BUT LESTER. YOU JUST FINISHED MAKING EXPERT LOVE TO ME WHILE GUNNING DOWN NINJAS.

OKAY, SURE. BUT MY HEART WASN'T IN IT.

BUT LESTER. DON'T YOU FIND ME DESIRABLE?

THERE WAS NOTHING I COULD DO FOR HER. ALL I FOUND WAS A TOOTH.

AND TO MAKE MATTERS WORSE, MY COPY OF THE RED PONY WAS IN FLAMES.

THERE WAS NOTHING LEFT FOR ME HERE.

I SET MY COURSE FOR MARIN. THE NIGHT HAD CLEARED, AND THE STARS TWINKLED WETLY, AS IF THEY TOO WEPT FOR THE POOR BRAVE GIRL WHO HAD GOTTEN HER WISH.

SOMEWHERE A BELL TOLLED. AND, BROTHER, YOU CAN BET I DIDN'T ASK FOR WHOM!

NEXT MONTH: **PICNIC!**

BOOP · BOOP · BOOP · BOOP · BOO

THE SONAR WOKE ME UP AGAIN.

SEEMS LIKE EVERY TIME I SLEEP IN MY MARIN COUNTY HOUSEBOAT THE SONAR WAKES ME UP

THAT'S WHY I HAD CUBAN DICK RIG UP AN AQUAZOOKA FOR ME.

BUT FIRST THINGS FIRST.

SPLASH!

IT WAS ANOTHER NUCLEAR SUB. I COULD TELL BY THE WAY IT SAT IN THE WATER THAT IT WAS ABOUT TO FIRE ON MY HOUSEBOAT.

1

BA-ZOOOOOSH

BOOM!

IT DEFLATED LIKE A FOOTBALL.

AND I STILL HAD TIME FOR COFFEE.

BUT ONLY FOR ONE CUP. THIS WAS THE BIG DAY. I HAD TO GET GOING.

BOY, A PERFECT DAY FOR IT, TOO.

GREAT. TRAFFIC'S LIGHT. I SHOULDN'T HAVE ANY TROUBLE GETTING TO THE EAST BAY.

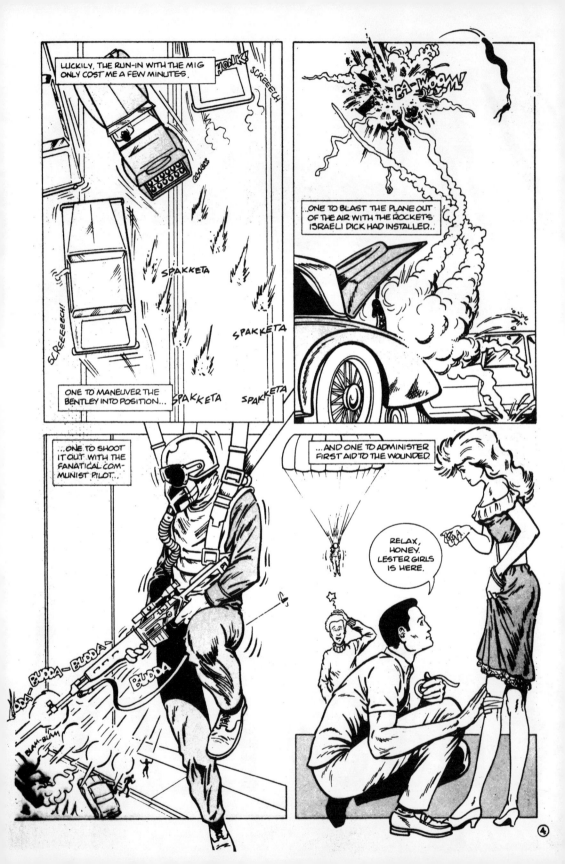

ARMENIAN SEPARATISTS. THEY'LL GET YOU EVERY TIME.

I DIDN'T MIND THE BENTLEY. IT WAS NEVER THE CAR I WANTED ANYWAY. IT WAS THE DELAY I COULDN'T AFFORD.

I CAME TO A BRITISH CAR LOT WITH A PHONE. BUT JUST AS I WAS DIGGING FOR A COUPLE OF DIMES...

EAST SIDE RULES

MR. GIRLS! MR. GIRLS! CONGRATULATIONS! AS THE MILLIONTH CUSTOMER ON OUR LOT, YOU ARE THE WINNER OF A BRAND NEW SLEEK, SILENT, SENSUOUS JAGUAR XJS!

DON'T YOU HAVE A NICE CHEVY STATION WAGON?

WHAT?!

SKIP IT.

HELL, SOMEDAY I'LL GET MY DREAM CAR. BUT I GUESS A JAG'S GOOD ENOUGH TO GET ME TO MY DESTINATION.

THANK YOU, MR. GIRLS! OH, THANK YOU, THANK YOU!

ORTS

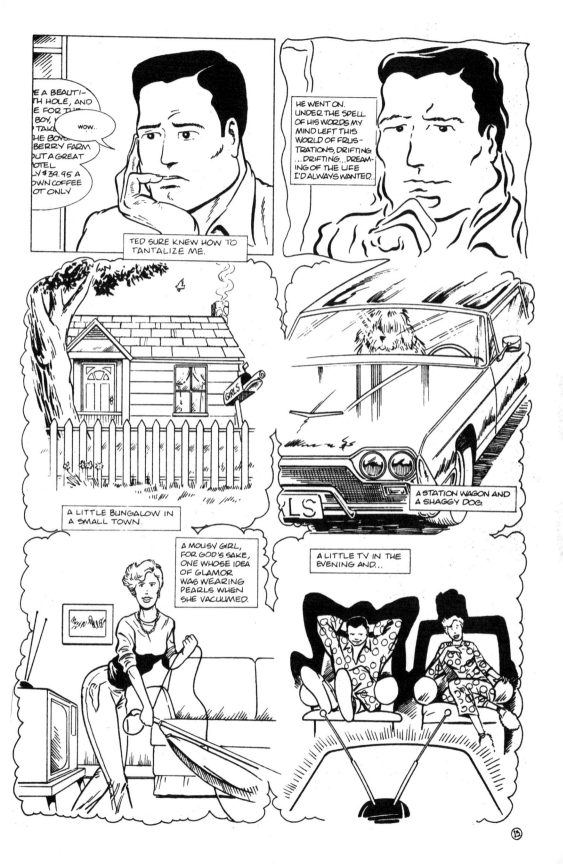

HI, WILLY! HI, JERRY!

HA, HA. CRAZY LADS.

HI, UNCLE LES!

WE GONNA KICK ASS IN THE SOFTBALL GAME?

OKAY! TIME TO PILE INTO THE PINTO, BOYS ...AND GIRLS!

GOOD OLD TED. HE ALWAYS LOVED THAT JOKE.

JESUS, LES. IS THAT A JAGUAR XJS?

'FRAID SO. BUT IT GETS ME AROUND.

MY HEART WAS RACING WHEN WE ARRIVED AT THE PARK.

LESTER, THIS IS BOB AND CAROLYN ...PETE AN' TILLIE... SAM AN' ELLA...

HI, FRIENDS! I SURE AM EXCITED TO BE HERE!

TED AND ALICIA'S FRIENDS SEEMED LIKE A LOVELY GROUP.

WHO'S HE TRYIN' TO KID?

WHAT A *HUNK!*

WHILE THEY PICKED TEAMS, THE BOYS AND I PEEKED INTO THE PICNIC BASKET.

OH BOY! BOLOGNA AND CHEESE SANDWICHES, FRITOS AND A JUG OF KOOL-AID!

UGH. NOT THAT CRAP AGAIN.

AH, THOSE BOYS HAVE A GREAT SENSE OF HUMOR.

IT WAS A BEAUTIFUL DAY, A BEAUTIFUL BUNCH OF PEOPLE, AND A BEAUTIFUL GAME.

BONK

BUT, AS ALWAYS, IT COULDN'T LAST.

WITH TWO OUTS IN THE NINTH INNING, OUR TEAM DOWN BY THREE RUNS AND THE BASES LOADED, IT HAD TO BE *MY* TURN AT BAT.

KRACK

WOULDN'T YOU KNOW IT? I HAPPENED TO CATCH THE SOFTBALL ON THE MEAT OF THE BAT...

AND DROVE IT UP ON THE FREEWAY ACROSS FROM THE PARK.

BUT *MR. GIRLS!* DON'T YOU WANT MONEY, FAME, AND THE CHANCE TO ENDORSE PRODUCTS ON NATIONAL TV?

LADY, ALL I WANT IS A GOOD NIGHT'S SLEEP.

BY THE TIME I GOT RID OF HIM I WAS IN A PRETTY SOUR MOOD. BUT AT LEAST I HAD THE DELICIOUS PICNIC LUNCH TO LOOK FORWARD TO.

OR SO I THOUGHT.

WAIT A MINUTE! THIS ISN'T OUR PIC-NIC BASKET!

DAMN. SOME CARELESS RICH FAMILY HAD ACCIDENTALLY SWITCHED BASKETS WITH US. INSTEAD OF ALICIA'S GREAT SPREAD, WE WERE STUCK WITH CANAPES, CAVIAR, SQUAB SANDWICHES AND DOM PERIGNON.

YOU'VE GOT TO HAND IT TO THE FOSTERS, THOUGH. THEY KEPT UP A GOOD FRONT, BRAVELY PRETENDING TO ENJOY THE MEAL.

I WAS PRETTY GLUM ON THE DRIVE BACK TO THEIR DUPLEX.

WHY SO QUIET, LES?

I DON'T KNOW. SEEMS LIKE EVERY TIME THINGS ARE LOOKING UP, SOMETHING'S GOTTA GO WRONG.

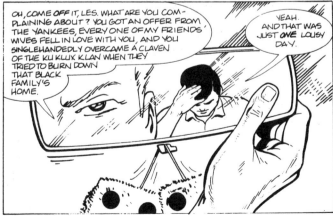

OH, COME *OFF* IT, LES. WHAT ARE YOU COMPLAINING ABOUT? YOU GOT AN OFFER FROM THE YANKEES, EVERY ONE OF MY FRIENDS' WIVES FELL IN LOVE WITH YOU, AND YOU SINGLEHANDEDLY OVERCAME A CLAVEN OF THE KU KLUX KLAN WHEN THEY TRIED TO BURN DOWN THAT BLACK FAMILY'S HOME.

YEAH. AND THAT WAS JUST *ONE* LOUSY DAY.

BUCK UP, LES! IF YOU WANT TO CHANGE YOUR LIFE, ALTHOUGH HEAVEN KNOWS WHY YOU WOULD, YOU OUGHT TO DO SOMETHING ABOUT IT, NOT JUST JET AROUND THE WORLD MOPING. WHY, LOOK AT ME. WHEN I WAS TEN POUNDS OVERWEIGHT I PUT MYSELF ON A CRASH DIET AND LOST IT ALL IN ONE MONTH.

I WISH IT WAS THAT EASY, ALICIA. BUT EVERYTIME I REACH FOR MY DREAMS I GET CAUGHT UP IN SOME NEW ACTION-PACKED ADVENTURE.

IT'S HOPELESS. HOPELESS.

COME ON, UNCLE LES!

YOU CAN DO ANYTHING YOU WANT!

MAYBE IT WAS HEARING THE BOYS SAY IT THAT GOT TO ME.

BUT SUDDENLY I KNEW THAT IT WAS TIME TO TRY AGAIN, TRY AS I NEVER HAD BEFORE.

HEAR THAT WORLD? I'M NOT BEATEN YET. THIS IS LESTER TALKING, WORLD! LESTER GIRLS! YES, FOR ONE LAST TIME, LESTER GIRLS WILL FIGHT FOR HIS DREAMS!

next issue: JOB HUNT

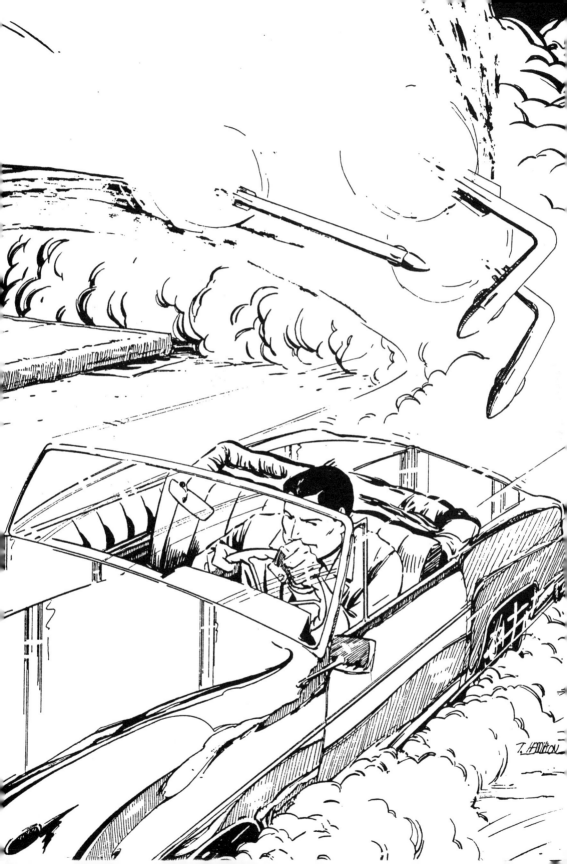

NEXT MORNING'S PAPER WAS A PLEASANT SURPRISE. NO BOMB WRAPPED IN IT...

...NO PARALYSIS GAS SEEPING UP FROM THE PAGES...

...NO CURARE ON THE EDGES...

CHINESE FIGHT FOR THEIR LIVES!

WHAT A PLEASANT WAY TO START THE DAY. I FLIPPED EAGERLY TO THE CLASSIFIEDS.

1.

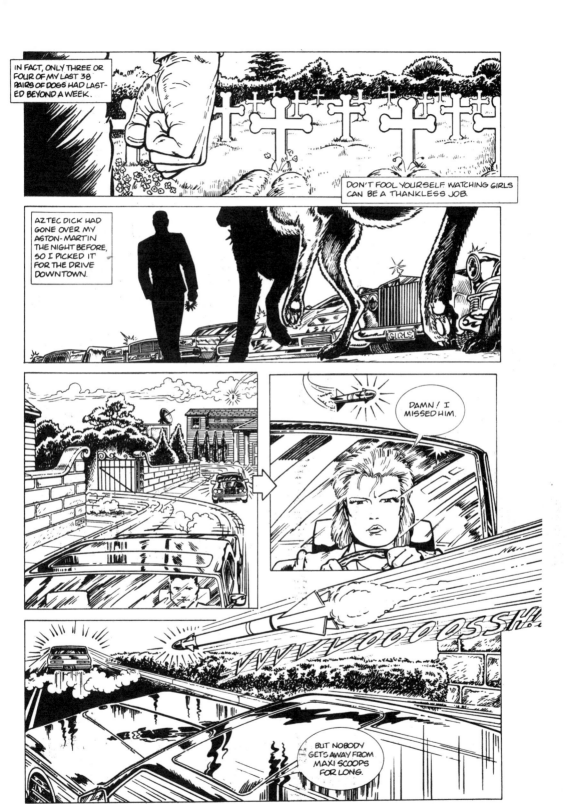

the INCREDIBLE

WHAT TH--?

I TRIED SHAKING IT...

GOOD OLD ASTON-MARTINS. SURE, EVERY CAR COMES WITH A RADIO, AND SEAT BELTS, AND A CIGARETTE LIGHTER. A LOT OF THEM EVEN HAVE SUN ROOFS.

BUT ONLY ASTON-MARTINS COME WITH CUSTOM EJECTION SEATS.

I SPOTTED A FLAGPOLE...

...PLOTTED MY TRAJECTORY...

...AND...

VOOSH!

FORTUNATELY, THE LITTLE CHILDREN PLAYING AN INNOCENT GAME OF HOP-SCOTCH WERE UNHURT.

SLICK MOVE. LOOKS LIKE HE REALLY *IS* EVERYTHING THEY SAY.

PERFECT. NO WAY HE'LL GET A *CAB* IN THIS PART OF TOWN. I'LL OFFER HIM A RIDE.

WITH MY TRAINING AS AN ACE REPORTER, I'LL HAVE HIS LIFE STORY BEFORE HE KNOWS WHAT'S HAPPENING.

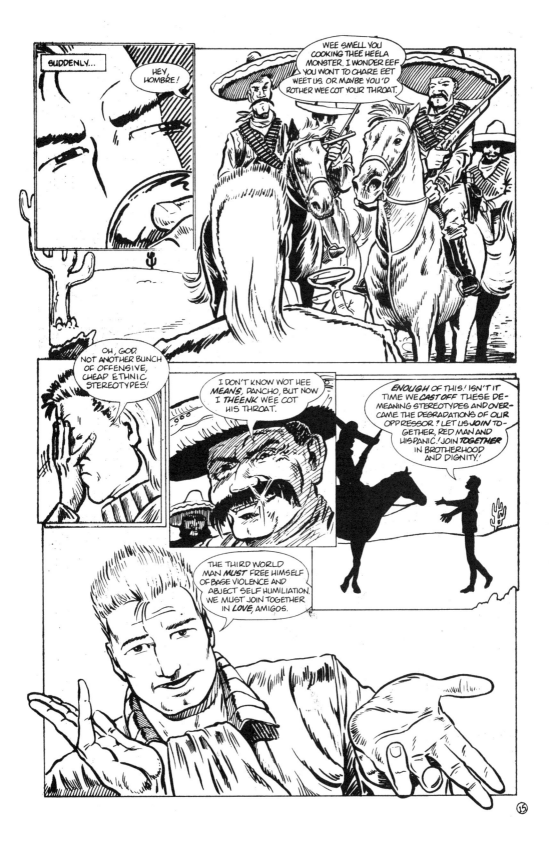

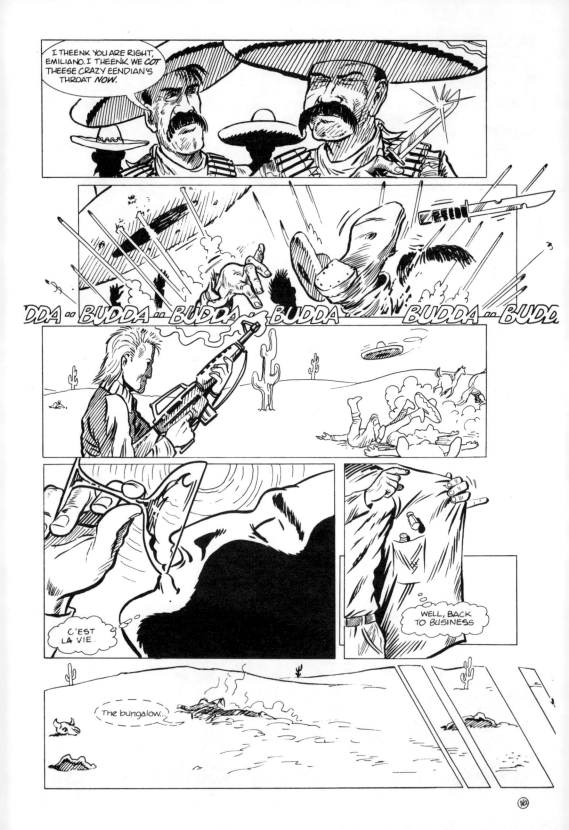

IT WASN'T UNTIL I WAS SOARING OVER THE BAY THAT I REALIZED I HADN'T THOUGHT ABOUT LANDING.

OH WELL. SOMETIMES YOU JUST HAVE TO WING IT.

THE CITY. HOW ITS STREETS BECKON TO THE LOST, THE LONELY, THE DE-FEATED. TO THEM THE FOG SEEMS TO WHISPER, "LAY YOUR BURDEN DOWN. I WILL COVER YOU LIKE A SOFT, GRAY SHROUD."

ALL THE LONELY PEOPLE. WHERE DO THEY ALL COME FROM? IT MATTERS NOT WHEN THEY ARE SWALLOWED UP IN THE COLD GRIM CANYONS OF... THE CITY.

THE CITY. POETS HAVE WRITTEN ABOUT IT. COMIC BOOK WRITERS, IN THEIR OWN WAY, HAVE ALSO TRIED BUT NO MAN'S WORDS CAN CAPTURE IT LIKE THE IMAGE OF A SINGLE BROKEN WOMAN.

ESPECIALLY WHEN SHE'S CUTE.

CHRIST. WHAT DO I DO *NOW*? THE BIGGEST SCOOP OF MY CAREER IS SOMEWHERE IN THIS *DUMP* OF A CITY AND *I'VE* LOST HIM. COMPLETELY.

NOT "CURLS," YOU *IDIOT!* GIRLS! LESTER GIRLS!

next issue: **THE STORY THAT HAD TO BE TOLD**
the **ORIGIN of LESTER GIRLS!!**

THE TROUBLE WITH GIRLS
The Novel

For you literary archivists out there, here are the first three chapters from the original Lester Girls novel, which we've adapted into the three installments you have just read.

CHAPTER ONE

Will He Shoot The Colt?

I was reading *The Red Pony* when the bombs went off. Luckily I was reading on the throne, not in bed where they expected me to be. On the way out of the apartment I stepped over the body of the Arab who'd driven the truck through the bedroom wall. I hailed a taxi and had it drive me to the corner of Geary and Lombard. As far as I could make out, only four cars followed. I zig-zagged through Union Square, burst into the Hyatt lobby, emerged through a service door on the Chinatown side, and hailed another cab. This time my old pal Screechy O'Herlihy was behind the wheel.

"Shaking another tail, Les?"

"Uh huh," I said, staring out the back of the cab.

"KGB? CIA? SS?"

"And PLO."

He dropped me off at my penthouse on Russian Hill. "Don't let your meat loaf, Les," he quipped.

Jesus, I thought. If only I could, for just one night.

I'd never seen the blonde who was curled up on my sofa before. She was wearing tight white ducks and a scarlet tube top. She looked at me over her glass and asked, "What kept you, Les?"

I don't know how they all knew my name, but I was getting used to it. "What do you know about the truck-bomb over on Union Street?" I asked.

In response she ran her tongue along the edge of the glass and asked if I wanted a wallbanger.

I said, "Not now. I want to read."

She said, "You want to do what, honey?"

I didn't want an argument, so I went in the bedroom and closed the door. I'd lost my book en route, but I always keep a copy of whatever I'm reading in all my houses, just in case. Unfortunately the one here was a different edition, so it took me ten minutes to find my place. God-damned Arabs.

Thankfully, the beautiful big-breasted blonde left me alone for a while. She turned the radio on and blared Prince at me, but at least she didn't barge into the room in the buff.

I was reading the part where Billy had to shoot the colt, but the assassination attempt had me so annoyed I couldn't concentrate. After reading the same paragraph three times I gave up and threw the book down in disgust.

I walked over to the window and looked down. There were six cars now. How did I know they didn't just belong to my neighbors? I guess after a while you can just tell, is all.

I threw open the window and hurled a heavy paperweight, striking the white Rolls smack on the hood. The Ugandan agents leapt out jabbering. Screw 'em.

The blonde was dancing by herself in the middle of my Navajo rug. She purred, "Did you change your mind about that drink, honey?"

"Why the hell not?" I said.

She never took her eyes off me while she poured the drink. She kicked her shoes off before she brought it to me, but even then she came up to my chin. She was a big girl.

"Taste it," I said.

"What?"

"You heard me, " I said. Last time one of these girls had mixed me a wallbanger, Apache Dick had to pump my stomach.

But this babe was on the level. She took a sip and then handed it over. "So what do you want from me?" I asked.

"Why do you say that, you big dreamy hunk?"

I chuckled softy and said, "Everybody wants somethimg from me, baby."

She ran her tongue over her moist lips and hooked a pinkie on my belt. I looked down, but I couldn't see her hand past the swell of those breasts. I put my free hand around her waist. And then the lights went out.

I threw us both to the floor. "Keep quiet," I hissed.

I crawled to the sofa, reached under the cushion, and pulled out my Llama Comanche II .38 Special with the high-polish deep blue finish. I could see their silhouettes through the windows, creeping along the ledge. They moved as silently as cats, their swords like raised tails.

When the blonde spoke, there was terror in her voice. "Who are they?" she stammered.

I said, "Ever hear of the Bushido Blade?"

Her "what?" was a throaty whisper.

"Skip it," I said, and cocked the revolver.

They had disappeared from the windows. For now.

I drew the girl into the middle of the room with me. I said, "They might come from anywhere."

I felt her trembling beside me. I put my arm around her and said, "Relax. You're with Lester Girls now."

She snuggled a little closer. Then her tongue was in my mouth. Danger excites them. The tube top slid off like an old sock. I let her undress me so I could keep a look-out. I thought I saw a shadow cross my Warhol, but I couldn't be sure.

When her ducks came off I could feel the wetness. It was hard keeping my head up. She moaned when I went in. I clamped a big hand over her mouth. Those Japanese have better hearing than dogs. Her moans turned to a steam bath against my palm.

The first one came in through the dumbwaiter with a flash of steel. I was careful to keep my gun away from the girl's face as I pumped three slugs into him.

The girl mumbled, "Don't stop."

I didn't. The second one swung through the window as she orgasmed again. I only spent two slugs on him because the blonde wasn't going to give me time to reload. It was enough. The second bullet caught him high in the chest and sent him hurtling back through the window. His piercing Oriental scream cleaved the night as he plummetted thirty stories.

I had two shots left, but only one in my gun. I knew which one I'd have to shoot first.

Then the air was whistling. I heard

the throwing stars thud into the Marantz console behind my head. I calculated the trajectory of the stars and fired into the darkness. The body fell amid shattering china.

The blonde came a fourth time and I fired my seventh shot.

Afterward, we tidied up a bit, mixed a couple of Kahlua toddies, and threw the bodies out the window. It was street cleaning night on 9th Avenue.

The blonde's name turned out to be Bibi MacNamara. She wanted me to talk to Solly Greenblatt about casting her opposite Arnie Schwarzenegger in some new movie they were making down in Tinseltown. I told her I didn't talk to Solly anymore. I didn't tell her about Mrs. Greenblatt. The room cooled noticeably.

She wanted to spend the night anyway, but I was anxious to get back to *The Red Pony*. So I peeled a couple of hundreds off my roll and showed her the door. She offered to go down on me again, but I just had to find out if Billy Buck shot that colt.

But wouldn't you know it? The silly girl had accidentally thrown out my book along with the bodies. There was only one thing to do. I strapped on my jet-pack and flew out the window. I knew I had a copy on my houseboat in Marin.

CHAPTER TWO

Girls Can Dream Too

A nuclear sub woke me up around dawn. I shut off the sonar, locked up the houseboat, and drove off in my Jag. Funny thing about the Jag. The day I'd gotten it I had set off to buy a nice used Pinto. But on the way to the Ford dealership some

Armenian separatists had shot out the tires of my Bentley with a bazooka. So I just happened to walk onto a British car lot to see if there was a phone I could use when this roly-poly salesman ran up to me yelling, "Mr. Girls! Mr. Girls! Congratulations! As the millionth customer to enter our lot you have won a brand-new sleek, silent, sensuous Jaguar XJ-S!"

Hell. Someday I'd get me a nice Pinto. But in the meantime, I guess the Jag was good enough to get me to Ted and Alicia's.

Let me tell you about my friends Ted and Alicia Foster. Ted's an assistant manager for a shoe store and Alicia, his lovely plain wife, is a clerk in the municipal court in Oakland. They live in a charming duplex in the quaint little community of Walnut Creek. Just recently they finished paying off their 19" color TV set and they've just invested in a matched pair of La-Z-Boy recliners. On Friday nights they always eat out at Shakey's.

God. I'd change places with them in a minute.

Yeah, a little peace and quiet, that's all I'd ever wanted. You know, a little bungalow in a small town. A station wagon and a shaggy dog. A mousy girl, for God's sake, one whose idea of glamour was wearing pearls when she vacuumed. A little TV in the evening and some hot milk at bedtime.

And then work. A quiet bus ride to the office, then a full eight hours balancing accounts and filling up the columns of the ledger. I could see it so clearly. A soft light, a comfy old cardigan, and, just beyond the door, the quiet chatter of the office gals.

But not this lad. What was I stuck with? High adventure and insatiable women.

It was a pretty smooth trip to the East Bay, except for the MiG strafing the Golden Gate Bridge. But even that only cost me a few minutes: One to blow the MiG out of the sky with the rockets Apache's cousin Hopi Dick had installed in the Jag, and a few more to drive the wounded Sunday motorists to the hospital.

Ted jumped up from the funny pages to let me in. We exchanged warm greetings, and Alicia served up mugs of hot, delicious instant coffee. As we settled onto the La-Z-Boys, Alicia asked, "How did your date with Mary Ellen go, Les?"

Ah, Mary Ellen Roberts, my ideal woman. The frumpy little darling who, last Saturday, I had finally managed to take out on a date.

"Oh, she's a little peeved at me," I sighed. "I took her to McDonald's the other day and three Parisian models on their lunchbreak came over squealing and crawled under my side of the table. And you know how women can be. She got the goofy idea that there was something between us."

Ted gave me a look I couldn't quite figure and said, "You sure got it tough, Les."

"Oh, what the hell," I said, suddenly embarrassed at the whine in my voice. "I guess I'm not the only guy with problems."

Alicia suddenly chirped, "You boys finish your coffee while I get the picnic lunch ready," and ran to the kitchen.

While she was gone, Ted tantilized me with stories about the shoe store, his golf scores, and his and Alicia's plans to take the boys to Disneyland. I could've listened to him all day, but all too soon it was time to leave for the softball game.

We found the boys, Willy and Jerry, chasing each other around the bushes when we stepped outside. Ted looked on warmly as I patted the kids on the head, and then he called, "Okay, boys and Girls, time to pile into the station wagon."

Good old Ted. He always loved that joke.

A lot of Ted and Alicia's friends were already at the park when we got there. While the Fosters ran over to greet them, the boys and I took advantage of the opportunity to peek into the picnic basket. To my joy, the sight of bologna and cheese sandwiches, Fritos, and a jug of Kool-Aid greeted my eyes.

"Ugh, not that shit again," Willy said.

Ah, those boys have a great sense of humor.

It was a beautiful day, a beautiful bunch of people, and a beautiful game. But, as always, it couldn't last. With two outs in the ninth inning, our team down by three runs and the bases loaded, I happened to catch the softball on the meat of the bat and drove it up onto the freeway that was across from the park. Being the hero of the game I didn't mind so much, but a few minutes later a limousine cruised up with its windshield shattered.

A stocky guy got out and yelled, "Who hit that ball?"

Willy and Jerry immediately pointed at me and shrilled, "Uncle Les did! Uncle Les did!"

I felt myself blushing as I peeled off a few hundreds from my roll. I approached the guy to pay him for his windshield, but he was just staring over the center field fence, ignoring me.

"Jesus, man," he bellowed. "You musta hit that ball seven hundred feet."

Six of the wives piped in unison, "And that was the ninth one the gorgeous hunk has hit today, Mister!"

"Well, this is my lucky day," the stout man said. "You see, I'm a scout for the New York Yankees. How would you like a multi-million dollar contract to play outfield for us? We've been a little disappointed with Mattingly, Winfield, and Henderson lately."

It took me half an hour to get rid of the guy. He was very persistent, and it didn't help any that Ted and Alicia's crazy friends all sided with him. By the time he left I was in a pretty sour mood, but at least I had that delicious picnic lunch to look forward to.

But suddenly Alicia cried out, "Wait a minute! That's not our picnic basket!"

Wouldn't you know it? Some careless rich family had passed through the park and accidentally switched baskets with us. Instead of the great meal Alicia had made for us, we were stuck with lobster canapes, caviar, squab sandwiches, and magnums of champagne. You've got to hand it to the Fosters, though. They kept up a good false front, bravely pretending to enjoy the meal.

I was pretty glum on the drive back to their duplex that evening. Finally, Alicia asked me why I was so quiet.

"I don't know," I said. "It seems like every time things are looking up, something's got to wrong."

"Oh, come off it, Les!" Ted said angrily. "What are you complaining about? You got an offer from the Yankees, every one of my friends' goddamn wives fell in love with you, and you singlehandedly overcame a claven of the Ku Klux Klan when they tried to burn down that black family's home."

"Yeah," I said gloomily, "and that's just in one day."

"Buck up, Les," Alicia said. "If you want to change your life—although heaven knows.why you would—you ought to do something about it, not just jet around the world moping. Why, look at me. When I was ten pounds overweight I put myself on a crash diet and lost it in one month."

"Well..." I began.

"Come on, Uncle Les," the boys chimed. "You can do anything you want to do."

Maybe it was hearing the boys say it

that got to me. But suddenly I knew that it was time to try again, even though I'd tried a million times before.

Yes, for one last time, Lester Girls would fight for his dreams.

CHAPTER THREE

Is It A Plane?

Next morning's paper was a pleasant surprise. No bomb wrapped in it, no paralysis gas seeping up from the pages, no curare on the edges...what a pleasant way to start the day. I flipped eagerly to the Classified Ads.

The first few columns were pretty disappointing (you know how depressing it can be to look for a job in the Classified). But then I spotted it: The perfect job for me. Elevator operator at a senior citizens' apartment complex. Nothing to do all day but stand in a little cubicle and shoot the breeze with the old-timers. And the pay was great, too...five bucks an hour. Enough to live on, but nothing ostentatious.

I was reaching for the phone to answer the ad when it hit me. How could I take a chance like that? What if one of my enemies—the Lizard Lady, Bear Claw, or even the nefarious Kid Glove—should snip the cables when I was taking on a load at the top floor? Sure, I'd probably survive the fall, but I'd have the blood of all those innocents on my hands. I guess it just wasn't meant to be.

Another ad caught my eye for a second, but I had to dismiss it too. It was for a milk-man in a little suburban neighborhood. Sound pretty peaceful to you? Sure, but what happens when all those beautiful housewives who haven't embarked on high-powered careers yet try to seduce me? It's bad enough that Khadafy had a price on my head. I didn't need a lot of irate husbands coming after me too.

But finally, I found one that I couldn't see anything wrong with. Fitting room supervisor at a department store. The work was simple but it sounded challenging. What I had to do was make sure that people left the room with the same number of items they'd come in with. And if it was like most places, I'd be standing alone inside the little room, so I wouldn't have to deal with any beautiful, voracious shopgirls. The ad also said that there was plenty of overtime available. Great! Maybe if I could get enough twelve-hour shifts it would help me stay out of mischief.

It was a beautiful morning, and to make things even more pleasant my watch-dogs, Bulwer and Lytton, had only mangled one would-be assassin during the night. Unfortunately, they'd dragged him over to the flower bed and chewed on him there, and once again they'd ruined the petunias I'd been trying to raise.

Good old Bulwer and Lytton. They were rascals, but I loved 'em. I'd already had them six days. My last pair of watchdogs, Beecher and Stowe, had been poisoned after three days. In fact, only three or four of my last thirty-eight pairs of dogs had lasted beyond a week. Don't fool yourself. Watching Girls can be a thankless job.

Aztec Dick, another of Apache's cousins, had gone over my Aston-Martin for booby-traps just the night before, so I'd selected it for the drive downtown. But I'd no sooner pulled out of my Pacific Heights mansion and turned left on Mission than I looked in my rear-view mirror and saw it.

Not more than ten feet behind me sped a heat-seeking missle. I hit the accelerator but it accelerated with me. I tried shaking it, like a tail, but a few random lefts and rights had no effect. It was still with me, and getting closer.

There was only one thing to do.

Good old Aston-Martins. Sure, every car comes with a radio, and seat belts, and a cigarette lighter. A lot of them even have sun roofs. But only Aston-Martins come with custom ejection seats.

I was about to push the button when a doubt assailed me. Which would the heat-seeker follow, the roaring car or my hurtling body? I figure I'd better make sure. I whipped a bottle of Chivas out of the glove compartment and doused the back seat with it. Then I flicked a lit match over my shoulder. While the back seat blazed, I scanned the street for an overhanging flagpole. I spotted one, carefully plotted my trajectory, flipped the false lid off the geat shift, scooted over to the passenger seat, and hit the button.

From my safe perch on the flag pole, I watched the missile connect and the car go up in a blaze of fire and screaming shrapnel. Fortunately, the little children playing an innocent game of hopscotch on the sidewalk were unhurt.

I dropped from the pole and landed nimbly on my feet. I ran to the corner of Funston and 13th Avenue and flagged down the first cab that came along.

"Where to today, Les?" Screechy asked.

I told him, and Screechy spun a left onto the Great Highway. As we whizzed alongside the beach, I happened to glance out the window and saw a dozen figures in scuba gear rise out of the surf. Simultaneously they raised their spear guns and fired. Suction cups splattered against the cab windows like barnacles. All at once twelve cables, running from twelve suction cubs to twelve motorized winches, began to pull. The cab slowed, stopped, and then, slowly but inexorably, began to skid backwards, toward the pounding foam.

"Quick, Les," Screechy barked.

"There's a bus over there. If you jump out now you can catch it."

"Forget it, Screechy," I snarled. "This is my fight."

"Stow it," he said. "Maybe I ain't the smartest guy in the world, but I do know one thing: Wherever Lester Girls has got to go, it's important that he get there. Now beat it—and I don't mean your meat."

The steel in his voice stifled the argument in my throat. Our eyes met briefly, and some silent but profound understanding passed between us. Then I was out of the cab and running.

As I boarded the bus and glanced back, Screechy was fending off the twelve scuba divers with nothing but a tire-iron and a bellyful of guts. God love 'im.

The bus was hijacked by Polish labor terrorists. I tried the sewers after that, but I was blocked by alligators with weird electrical gadgets on their heads that were obviously mind-control devices. I was starting to wonder if I was ever going to get to that damned department store. I even tried renting a helicopter and lowering myself to the store's roof by grappling hook, but a crazy sniper had to pick that day to post himself there, and he mistook me for a cop.

Finally I knew there was only one thing left to do.

It only took me a half-hour to swim across the Bay. I remembered seeing the posters for the circus that was visiting Oakland, so I found it without any trouble. I cornered the ringmaster and explained my problem. He agreed to help, but on one condition: That I fill in for the trapeze artist who had fallen ill that morning.

The act went pretty smoothly, except that the audience took so long in giving their standing ovation that I was in a cold sweat by the time they wheeled the cannon out; I had only five minutes left to make my job interview. The guy manning the cannon objected furiously to my insistence that he pack an extra charge of explosive into it, but I peeled a few hundreds off my roll and he shut up quick. All that was left was to calculate the trajectory and crawl into the barrel.

It wasn't until I was soaring over the Bay Bridge that I realized I hadn't thought about landing. But sometimes you just have to wing it.

I must have been quite a sight when I walked into the personnel office. My shirt was shredded and my face was covered with soot and I'd forgotten to put my pants back on over the aerialist's outfit. I'd even lost one of my ostrich boots during the flight. But when I entered, the secretary smiled brightly and said, "Good afternoon, Mr. Girls. Step right into Mr. Drysdale's office."

The portly personnel manager hit me with a lot of tough questions, but I thought I made the right impression. I made it perfectly clear that I was a reliable hard-worker, that I wouldn't cause trouble, and that I'd quietly do my job without ever trying to step over anybody else. I told him that I didn't have any ambition to be anything more than a fitting room supervisor. At the end of it he smiled blandly and picked up the phone.

He spoke very softly, so I couldn't hear what he was saying, but he began smiling broadly, and when he finally hung up my hopes were soaring.

"Well, Mr. Girls," he said. "When can you start?"

"Right away," I said, beaming.

He chuckled good-naturedly and said, "Well, better wait 'till next Monday. That'll give the man you're replacing time to get all his personal effects out of the Lear Jet."

"I don't get it," I said.

"Why, Mr. Girls," he said. "Of course the president of the world's largest depart-

7

ment store chain needs his own plane."

"Wha—?"

"I just spoke to the Chairman of our Board of Directors in New York. Our stockholders voted you in unanimously as soon as they heard you were in my office."

I rose unsteadily to my feet.

"Is there a problem, Mr. Girls?" he asked, his brow knit worriedly.

I tried to speak but I couldn't.

"If it's about the jet, rest assured that, although we only lent it to your predecessor, in your case we would be only too happy if you'd accept it as a gift."

I wheeled around and ran the hell out of there.

To Be Continued...

AFTERWORD
Will Jacobs
Gerard Jones

The Trouble With Girls started out as a novel. We wrote the first nine chapters and sent it off to our agent. To make a long story short, he didn't know what the hell to make of it. He could think of no convenient pigeonhole into which it fit. Humor? Well, yes, but not nearly as *overtly* funny as our first book, *The Beaver Papers*. Action? Yes, it has action, to be sure, but who wants *funny* action? To market a book successfully, it seems, the subject matter must be easily classifiable. *The Trouble With Girls* didn't even come close.

We could have given up at that point, but we had grown too fond of Lester Girls and company by then to throw in the towel. What to do? Find another agent? Try to market it ourselves? Or...wait a minute. Wait just a minute! Why not turn *The Trouble With Girls* into a comic book?

Well, why the hell not? We've always loved comics. We have a good understanding of the medium as our second book, *The Comic Book Heroes,* might attest. And writing a comic book would certainly provide an interesting challenge. So why the hell not give it a whirl?

We promptly worked up a proposal and sent it to the kindly lads at *Eternity Comics*, Dave Olbrich and Tom Mason.

They liked it, they made us an offer, and before we knew it the time had come to get down to work.

And to make a very big decision.

In adapting a story from one medium to another, how many alterations should be made? Book readers are more sophisticated than comic book fans, correct? They're accustomed to a far wider range of subject matter, right? Isn't the comic book community a small, inbred subculture that demands formularized superhero fare month after month, and nothing but?

Well...maybe so. A trip to your local comic book store and a quick scan of the brightly-colored, fantasy-filled, action-packed covers might certainly suggest as much. So what to do? Simplify our story? Tone down the humor to make it more accessible? Toss in a dose of glorified violence every couple of pages? In short, adulterate our concept to fit it into the narrow demands of the medium?

No, sir.

Because we don't feel comic book readers are necessarily as narrow-minded as most comics on the stands might suggest. We believe comic book readers are limited only in the choices comic book publishers provide them with. So why contribute to this situation? Why not alter our material only in form, but not one whit in content? Why not show the fans a little respect rather than write *down* to their alleged limitations?

Sure. Why not?

This is not to suggest that *The Trouble With Girls* is supposed to be *Finnegan's Wake* or *The Magic Mountain*. It is not meant to imply that we possess a loftier orientation than the average comic book reader. It is meant only to illustrate that our orientiation is *different*, and that *different* is not necessarily the kiss of death in this medium.

The Trouble With Girls has enjoyed a respectable success in the world of comics. This is very gratifying to us for two reasons. We are pleased to have contributed to this fascinating art form we so dearly love. But more importantly, in not compromising our material, we are very happy that this book has also reached you, the non-comic book reading world.

Welcome, and do come see us in the pages of our comic.

Will Jacobs
Gerard Jones

"What in Sam Hill?" I yelled. "Who's doing the shooting?"

"It can't be the stewardess," Apache said. "She parachuted out twenty minutes ago to visit her aunt in Camarillo."

I unbuckled myself from the seat and shouldered my way aft. Machine gun bullets were still racketing outside the plane. The craft lurched when another MiG exploded a few inches away. I hurled myself at the hatch of the gunnery compartment, threw it open.

"Look at me, Uncle Les!" Willy and Jerry piped in chorus. "I'm a tailgunner! I'm a tailgunner!"

That split-second break in their tooth-gritting concentration proved disastrous. Before I could even open my mouth to scold those pesky stowaways a MiG pierced our defenses and stitched the side of the plane with .50 calibre slugs.

From *The Trouble With Girls* novel, Chapter 8, "Boys And Girls Together."

This is the scene that artist Tim Hamilton pencilled and inked as a test page prior to landing the assignment. This page appears in slightly altered form in *The Trouble With Girls* #7.

ALSO AVAILABLE FROM ETERNITY COMICS

ARGONAUTS
He's come from the future to save the past.
Bill Spangler/Patrick Olliffe
#1 SOLD OUT!
#2 $2.50

BATTLE TO THE DEATH
Aliens vs. Ninjas vs. Samurai
#2-3 $1.00ea

BIG PRIZE
Willis loved the '30s—until he was stuck there.
#1-2 $2.50ea

BLADE OF SHURIKEN
Reggie Byers
#1-5 $1.00ea

BLOODBROTHERS
A new *Bloodwing* mini-series by Bill Spangler.
#1 $2.50

BLOODWING
1200 years in the future, at the edge of known space...
#1-5 $2.50ea

BONES
So this is life after death?
#1-4 $1.00ea

BORDERGUARD
#1-2 $1.00ea

BUSHIDO
Members of the Asano Group—an organization of paranor-mals—are being systematically murdered. Bruce Balfour and Ben Dunn.
#1-2 $2.50ea

CARNAGE
#1 $1.00

CHINA SEA
Graphic Novel
From the creator of *Elflord* comes an epic saga of magic, murder, and adventure.
80-pages $6.00

COLLECTION
A young girl fights to save her planet from aliens in this 64-page sf graphic novel. $1.00

COSMIC HEROES
Buck Rogers, 25th Century A.D. returns to comics in this monthly collection of the classic strip from the '30s.
#1 $2.50

CRIME CLASSICS
The Shadow returns in this monthly collection of the classic comic strip from the '40s.
#1-3 $2.50ea

DARK WOLF
R.A. Jones and Butch Burcham (Mini-Series)
#1 $6.00   #2-4 $3.00ea
(Regular Series)
#1 $3.00   #2-4, 6-8 $2.50ea

DARK WOLF COLLECTION
The complete mini-series plus the first Dark Wolf story ever. Introduction by Archie Goodwin.
$8.00

DEATH HUNT
#1 $1.00

DINOSAURS FOR HIRE
Extinct? No. Armed and Dangerous? Yes! #1 $5.00
#2-4 $2.50ea
Fall Classic
#1 $3.00

DRAGONFORCE
Super-Heroes, the Aircel Way, by Dale Keown.
#5-6 $2.50ea

EDGAR ALLAN POE
Classic illustrated tales of terror by the master.
The Tell-Tale Heart & Other Stories $2.50
The Pit And The Pendulum $2.50

ELFLORD
Hawk searches for the mysterious island of white-haired elves.
Barry Blair
#23-24 $2.50ea

EMPIRE
SF adventure
#1-4 $1.00ea

EX-MUTANTS (Original Series)
#1(Signed/Ron Lim) $10.00 ea
#6-7 $2.50 each

EX-MUTANTS
Graphic Novel Volume One:
The Saga Begins
96pp. $8.00
Graphic Novel Volume Two:
Gods Or Men
96 pp. $8.00

EX-MUTANTS: The Shattered Earth Chronicles
All new! The adventures of everybody's favorite former mutants.
#1 $3.00 #2-5 $2.50ea
Annual #1 $3.00

EX-MUTANTS PIN-UP BOOK
Full color pin-ups by Ron Lim.
#1 $3.00

FIST OF GOD
The Saga Of
Mick Taggert
From the bars of El Paso to the desert sands of Persia, Taggert must rescue the woman he loves.
#1 SOLD OUT!
#2-3 $2.50ea

FRIGHT
Classic tales of terror
#1-2, 4 $2.50ea
#3 (Nightmare On Elm Street cover) $3.00

GAMBIT
Alien adventures aboard the starship Gambit by Scott Bieser.
#1 $2.50

G.I. MUTANTS
Mutant Commandos.
#1-4 $1.00ea

GONAD
Full color barbarian adventures by Madman.
#1 $1.00

HUMAN GARGOYLES
Gargoyles battle Satan.
#1-2 $2.50ea

INVISOWORLD
#1 $1.00

KIKU SAN
The new *Elflord* spinoff title by Barry Blair.
#1-2 $2.50ea

LIBRA
Japanese style super-hero by Delfin Barral.
#1 $1.00

LIBBY ELLIS
Dennis Pimple and Norm Dwyer
#1 $3.00
2-4 $2.50ea
#1-2, 4 (New Series) $2.50ea

LIBERATOR
Super-heroes invade Nicaragua!
O'Connor, Chadwick, & Butch (*Dark Wolf*) Burcham. Jerry Bingham cover on #1.
#1-2, #4 $2.50 ea
#3 SOLD OUT!

LUNATIC BINGE
Madman's tales of Halloween horror.
#1 $1.00

MIGHTY MITES
#1-2 $1.00ea

NAZRAT
#6 $1.00

NEW HUMANS
Shattered Earth
The first **Ex-Mutants** spin-off! Full color covers by Ron Lim on #1 and #2. (40 pages each). The Sea Horse Saga begins in issue #6 with the introduction of all new characters.
#1 $3.00 #2-7 $2.50ea

NINJA
Meet the Red Dog Team...when all reason fails.
#1-2, 6-7, 9-10 $1.00ea
Special #1 (40 pp) $1.00

NINJA FUNNIES
#2-5 $1.00ea

NINJA HIGH SCHOOL
128-page graphic novel collecting the first three issues the acclaimed comic with a brand new 26-page story done especially for this volume.
First Printing $10.00

Second Printing $8.00
(Signed and numbered by Ben
Dunn) $15.00
(Limited
availability)

NINJA HIGH SCHOOL
Follow the gang from Quagmire
High in all-new adventures by
Ben Dunn!
#5-7 $2.50ea
#1 (60 pp) $3.50
#2 (40 pp) $2.50
#3 (40 pp) $2.50

OUTLANDER
Adam Gallow is on the run from
the Institute that trained and
manipulated him.
From the writer and artist of **War
Of The Worlds!**
#1-7 $2.50ea

PELLESTAR
#1-2 $1.00ea

PIRATE CORPS.
Evan Dorkin
#1-4 $1.00ea

PRIVATE EYES
The Saint returns in this
collection of his '50s strips by
Leslie Charteris and John
Spranger.
#1-2 $2.50ea

PROBE
Frank Turner's sf adventure
series.
#2-3 $1.00ea

RETROGRADE
It's not just their name, it's
what's happening to them.
Illustrated by Frank Turner.
#1, #3 $1.00ea

ROBOTECH II:
THE SENTINELS
At last! The sequel to Macross
arrives in comic book form. Tom
Mason/Chris Ulm/Jason and
John Waltrip.
#1 $2.50 (40 pp)
#2 $2.50 (40 pp)
Full color poster $6.95

ROVERS
In a post-
holocaust future, high school
students hold parttime jobs—as
bounty hunters.
S.A. Bennett/Scott Bieser/Mike
Roberts
#1-7 $1.00ea

SAMURAI
Hotachi Kimura (Samurai)
returns to wreak havoc on the
forces of SPLINTER. Created by
Barry Blair.
#2 $2.50

SCARLET IN GASLIGHT
Sherlock Holmes & Dracula! A
four-issue series by Martin
Powell and Seppo Makinen.
Supply is very limited!
#1, #4 $4.00ea
#2-3 SOLD OUT!

SCARLET IN GASLIGHT
Graphic Novel
Collects all four issues of the
acclaimed mini-series—
complete with rare pre-
production sketches.
$8.00

SCIMIDAR
In the year 2005, she stalks the
night. Written by R.A. Jones, co-
creator of *Dark Wolf* and *Fist Of
God*. #3 introduces penciller
Rob Davis.
#1 (Lim cover) $2.50
#2-3 (Balent cover) $2.50ea

SHANGHAIED
#2-3 $1.00ea

SHATTERED EARTH
Tales of the Ex-Mutants
Universe
#1 $2.50

SHERLOCK HOLMES
The classic strip from the '50s
collected for the first time.
Written by Edith Meiser and
illustrated by Marvel Comics
veteran Frank Giacoia. Dailies
and Sundays, complete and
uncut.
#1 $3.00 #2-5 $2.50ea

SHURIKEN TEAM-UP
#1 $1.00

SOLO EX-MUTANTS
Shattered Earth
The Ex-Mutants star in new solo
adventures.
#1 (Erin) $3.00 40 pp
#2 (Vikki) $2.50 40pp
#3 (Angela) SOLD OUT!
#4 (Doc) $2.50 40pp
#5 (Erin) $2.50 40pp

SPICY
DETECTIVE STORIES
Graphic Novel
The spiciest detective fiction of
the '30s, complete with original
illustrations.
96 pages
$8.00

SPICY TALES
Classic uncensored tales of
Bondage, Murder, and
Seduction from the '30s.
#1-3 $3.00ea

STARLIGHT
The Outer Space Babes.
#1 $1.00

STEALTH FORCE
They're back from the dead and
mad as hell!
#1-7 $1.00ea

TIGER-X
A Soviet invasion has split
America in half.
From Ben Dunn, the creator of
Ninja High School.
Special #1 SOLD OUT!
#1 (regular issue) $2.50
#2 SOLD OUT!
#3 (regular issue)
$2.50

TROUBLE WITH GIRLS
Nothing satisfies like *Girls!*
#1-$6.00   #2-4 $3.00ea
#8-9, 11-13 $2.50ea
Annual #1 (60pp) $3.50
#5-7,#10 SOLD OUT!

TWILIGHT AVENGER
He's back! The costumed
avenger from the '30s returns in
all new adventures by John
Wooley and Terry Tidwell.
#1-4 $2.50ea

VAMPYRES
They stalk the night with but one
thing on their undead minds—
your blood.
#1 $2.50 (40pp)

VERDICT
He hunts a killer known as The
Lunatik. Martin Powell and Dean
Haspiel.
#1 (Chaykin cover) $3.00
#2-3 $2.50ea

VICTIMS
Innocent girls are captured and
tortured by an unknown evil.
#1-2 $2.50ea

WAR OF THE WORLDS
The Aliens have landed in this
all-new adaptation of the classic
H.G. Wells novel by Scott Finley
and Brooks Hagan.
#1 $2.50

WARLOCKS
#2 $2.50

WILD KNIGHTS
Shattered Earth
From the pages of *Ex-Mutants*
to the highways of the Shattered
Earth!
Evan Dorkin, Alex Leonine, and
Dan Panosian.
#1 $3.00
#2-5 $2.50ea

All prices include postage
(US orders only—Canada
and Mexico add $1.00 per
order, Overseas add $2.00
per order). Comics are
shipped in plastic bags within
two weeks of receipt of
order. Please list alternates if
possible.

Send orders and make
checks payable to:
MALIBU GRAPHICS
PO Box 3185-A
Thousand Oaks, CA 91359

THE ALIENS HAVE LANDED!

WAR OF THE WORLDS

Based On The Novel by H.G. WELLS

Written by
Scott Finley
Illustrated by
Brooks Hagan

Every
Other
Month
From
ETERNITY

THE TWILIGHT AVENGER

He's Back!

From ETERNITY

EX-MUTANTS

In the year 2025, Australia is no longer "the wonder down under."

DESERT FOX ™

DESERT FOX
An *Ex-Mutants* Universe Title

From ETERNITY

Illustration by Jim Balent and Doug Hazlewood.

elflord

The Quest For
The Isle Of
White-Haired Elves Continues

Created, Written, and Illustrated by Barry Blair
Every Month From AIRCEL

Shortly after World War I,
Buck Rogers was trapped in
an abandoned mine and felled
by a mysterious gas.

When he awoke, he found
himself in a world of ray guns,
rocket belts, flying women and
mongol invaders.

Welcome home, Buck Rogers.
Welcome to the 25th Century.

COSMIC HEROES
featuring *Buck Rogers, 25th Century A.D.*
The Classic Comic Strip From The '30s.
Written by Phil Nowlan
Illustrated by Dick Calkins

From ETERNITY

CRIME CLASSICS

The Classic
Shadow
Comic Strip
By Maxwell
Grant And
Vernon Greene
From The
1940s.

The Original
Shadow In
His Original
Form.

Every Month.

From
ETERNITY.